May God BLESS YOU and KEEP YOU

Written by SARAH RAYMOND CUNNINGHAM

Illustrated by LORIAN TU

beaming ☀ books

MINNEAPOLIS

In the morning, when you awake,
When you first open up your eyes,
When you first move and roll over
And stretch your arms and legs out wide,

May God bless you.
May God keep you.
May God's face shine on you today.

May God give you grace
And keep you safe.
May God be with you always.

At the table when you're eating,
When you pull on clothes today,

When you wash your face and brush your teeth
And head out on your way,

When you're going off to school,
When you're learning in your class,

When you're singing, drawing, painting,
When you are running through the grass,

May God bless you.
May God keep you.
May God's face shine on you today.
May God give you grace
And keep you safe.
May God be with you always.

When you're climbing on the playground,
When you're flying down the slide,
When you're spinning round and round,
When you are swinging to the sky,

May God bless you.
May God keep you.
May God's face shine on you today.
May God give you grace
And keep you safe.
May God be with you always.

When you're playing in your bedroom,
When toys are pouring out the door,
When you pretend and make believe
And read all stretched out on the floor,

When you're twirling at recitals
Or playing music for a crowd,

When you're reciting poetry
Or belting choir songs out loud,

May God bless you.
May God keep you.
May God's face shine on you today.

May God give you grace
And keep you safe.
May God be with you always.

When you're sitting still at church,
When you're squirming in the car,

When you're swimming in the water,
When you're running near and far,

When you're strong as strong can be,
When you're the bravest kid around,

When you're feeling sick and tired,
And when your problems get you down,

May God bless you.
May God keep you.
May God's face shine on you today.

May God give you grace
And keep you safe.
May God be with you always.

When you're getting along well,
When you are arguing a lot,

When you're hyper or you're cranky,
When you're happy or you're not,

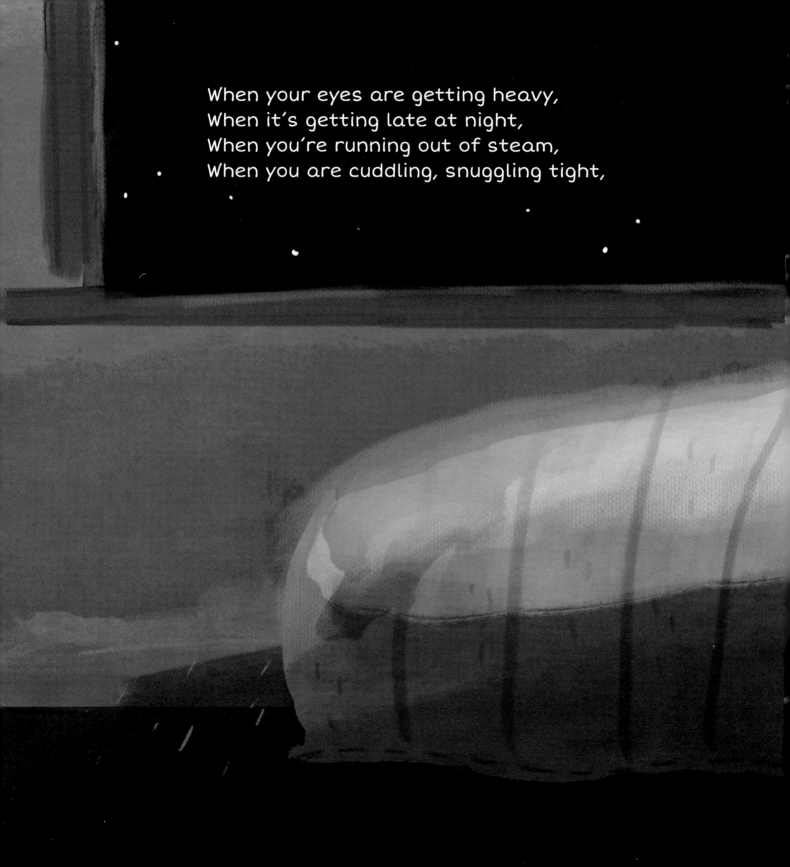

When your eyes are getting heavy,
When it's getting late at night,
When you're running out of steam,
When you are cuddling, snuggling tight,

May God bless you.
May God keep you.
May God's face shine on you today.
May God give you grace
And keep you safe.
May God be with you always.

To my sons, Justus and Malachi. May God bless you and keep you both. —S.R.C.

For Mom and Dad, with love. —L.T.

24 23 22 21 20 19 18   1 2 3 4 5 6 7 8

ISBN: 9781506445311

Written by Sarah Raymond Cunningham
Illustrated by Lorian Tu
Design by Christa Schneider, Mighty Media, Inc.
Production by Lauren Williamson, 1517 Media

Library of Congress Cataloging-in-Publication Data

Names: Cunningham, Sarah Raymond, 1978- author.
Title: May God bless you and keep you / written by Sarah Raymond Cunningham ;
      illustrated by Lorian Tu.
Description: First edition. | Minneapolis : Beaming Books, 2018.
Identifiers: LCCN 2018013948 | ISBN 9781506445311 (hardcover : alk. paper)
Subjects: LCSH: Benediction—Juvenile literature. | Children—Religious
      life—Juvenile literature. | Children—Prayers and devotions—Juvenile literature.
Classification: LCC BV197.B5 C86 2018 | DDC 242/.62—dc23 LC record available at https://lccn.loc.gov/2018013948

VN0004589; 9781506445311; JUL2018

Beaming Books
510 Marquette Avenue
Minneapolis, MN 55402
Beamingbooks.com